Pete the Cat's
Groovy Guide to Life

Tips from a **COOL CAT**
for living an
AWESOME Life

by Kimberly
& James Dean

HARPER
An Imprint of HarperCollinsPublishers

For Camille Morgan. I am ever thankful for your advice
that I should draw a picture of my cat. (James 1:5)
—J.D.

For Martin Lucki—we've been through it all,
thank you for all the uplifting words! (Proverbs 19:20)
—K.D.

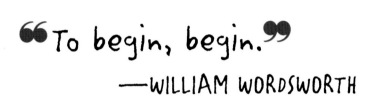

"To begin, begin."

—WILLIAM WORDSWORTH

any path will get you there." —LEWIS CARROLL

"Life is really simple,
but we insist on making it
complicated."

—CONFUCIUS

"Walking with a friend in the dark is

better than walking alone in the light.💬

—HELEN KELLER

"Opportunity is missed by most people because it comes dressed in overalls and looks like work."

—THOMAS EDISON

"You miss 100 percent of the shots you don't take."

—WAYNE GRETZKY

❝ When everything seems
to be going against you,
remember that an airplane
takes off against the wind,
not with it. **❞**

—HENRY FORD

"Be yourself. Everyone else is already taken."

—OSCAR WILDE

"Make each day your masterpiece."

—JOHN WOODEN

It's cool to color outside the lines!
—PETE
BLUE
GREEN
RED
YELLOW

"Every child is an artist.
The problem is how to remain
an artist once we grow up."

—PABLO PICASSO

"You must do the things you think you cannot do."

—ELEANOR ROOSEVELT

"Write it on your heart
that every day is the best
day in the year.**"**

—RALPH WALDO EMERSON

"A meowing cat catches no mice."

—YIDDISH PROVERB

"I have not failed. I've just found 10,000 ways that won't work."

—THOMAS EDISON

"Everybody is a genius. But if you judge a fish by its ability to climb a tree, it will live its whole life believing that it is stupid."

—ATTRIBUTED TO ALBERT EINSTEIN

"Hope is the thing with feathers
That perches in the soul,
And sings the tunes without the words,
And never stops at all."

—EMILY DICKINSON

"Most folks are as happy as they make up their minds to be."

—ABRAHAM LINCOLN

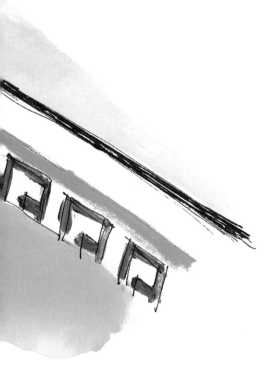

killful sailors." —PROVERB

"A man who carries a cat by the tail learns something he can learn in no other way."

—MARK TWAIN

"If music be the food of love, play on!"

—WILLIAM SHAKESPEARE

“Be kind whenever possible.
It is always possible.”

—DALAI LAMA XIV

**"A well-spent day
brings happy sleep."**

—LEONARDO DA VINCI